THE GRAPEFRUIT SEED

I would like to thank Janet Gray and Dale Neuschwander for all their help with grammar, spelling, and punctuation. I'll tayk ful rasponsibylity for eny mistayks.

* * * * * * * * * * * * * * *

Copyright © 1983 by Jim Ploof

Library of Congress Catalog Card Number

83-90126

ISBN   0-9611740-0-5

* * * * * * * * * * * * * * *

Printed in the United States of America

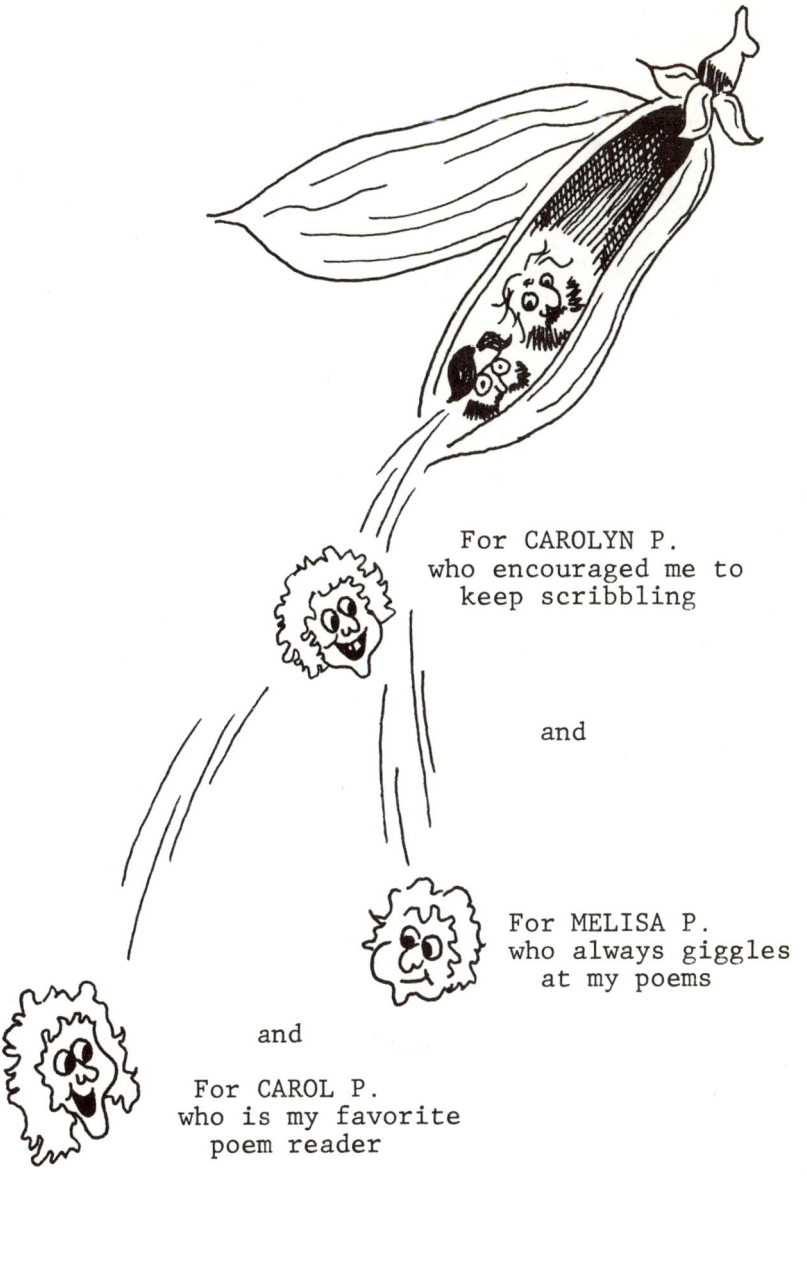

For CAROLYN P.
who encouraged me to
keep scribbling

and

For MELISA P.
who always giggles
at my poems

and

For CAROL P.
who is my favorite
poem reader

THE GRAPEFRUIT SEED

Today I cut into a grapefruit,
And as the knife went through
It cut a seed in half.
I wondered!!

If I planted that half-a-seed
Would it grow half-a-tree?
Would half-a-bird come along
And build half-a-nest,
And lay half-an-egg,
And hatch half-a-baby bird,
And feed it half-a-worm?

I think I'll run out
And plant this half-a-seed,
Cuz I just half-a-know!!

THE BALLOON

Once a kid bought a balloon
While at the county fair.
He had a string put on it
And he tied it in his hair.

Suddenly the wind came up.
The balloon went sailing high.
It pulled the kid right with it
Way up into the sky.

The balloon and that little kid
Traveled far and wide.
The kid was scared! He couldn't land
No matter how he tried.

So if you see a kid go by
Sailing high and free,
Try reaching up to grab him
Cuz that little kid is me.

MELISA'S ROOM

Melisa's room was such a mess
You couldn't find the floor,
And once you managed to get inside
You couldn't find the door.
You couldn't find the bed,
Or the dresser, or the chair.
You couldn't even find the walls
It was so bad in there.
In fact, her room was such a mess
And so very unappealing,

TOFFEE SQUARES

```
Carolyn loved toffee squares,
One at a time,
And also in pairs.
She ate them for breakfast
And dinner and lunch.
She ate them all day.
She ate by the bunch.
The doctor said if she didn't quit
She'd soon be six feet in the ground.
So what did she do to solve this dilemma?
Simple!!   Now she eats toffee rounds!
```

MR. SNOON

Old man Snoon taught English.
He was a real grumpy old bear.
Sometimes you'd swear he'd kill ya
If you fooled around in there.

One day a boy was throwin'
Spitballs all over the place.
Old man Snoon went back there
And rearranged his face.

Another day a little kid
Was screamin' in the hall.
Old man Snoon just grabbed her neck
And smashed her through the wall.

He caught a student sound asleep
At his desk right in the room.
How I wish you could have seen
Just how far old Snoony threw'm!

Frank stuck Susie with a pin.
You shoulda heard Sue holler!!
Snoon kicked their butts so doggone hard,
Now they're both three inches taller.

A kid named Al had a reputation
For bein' a real big talker.
Old Snoony took him in the hall
And crammed him in a locker.

Ya, Snoon was getting much too mean.
Something had to be done!
The student body was decreasin'
One, by one, by one.

Well, at eleven-thirty I took some honey
And poured it over Snoon.
And a real bear came in our school
And ate him for lunch at noon.

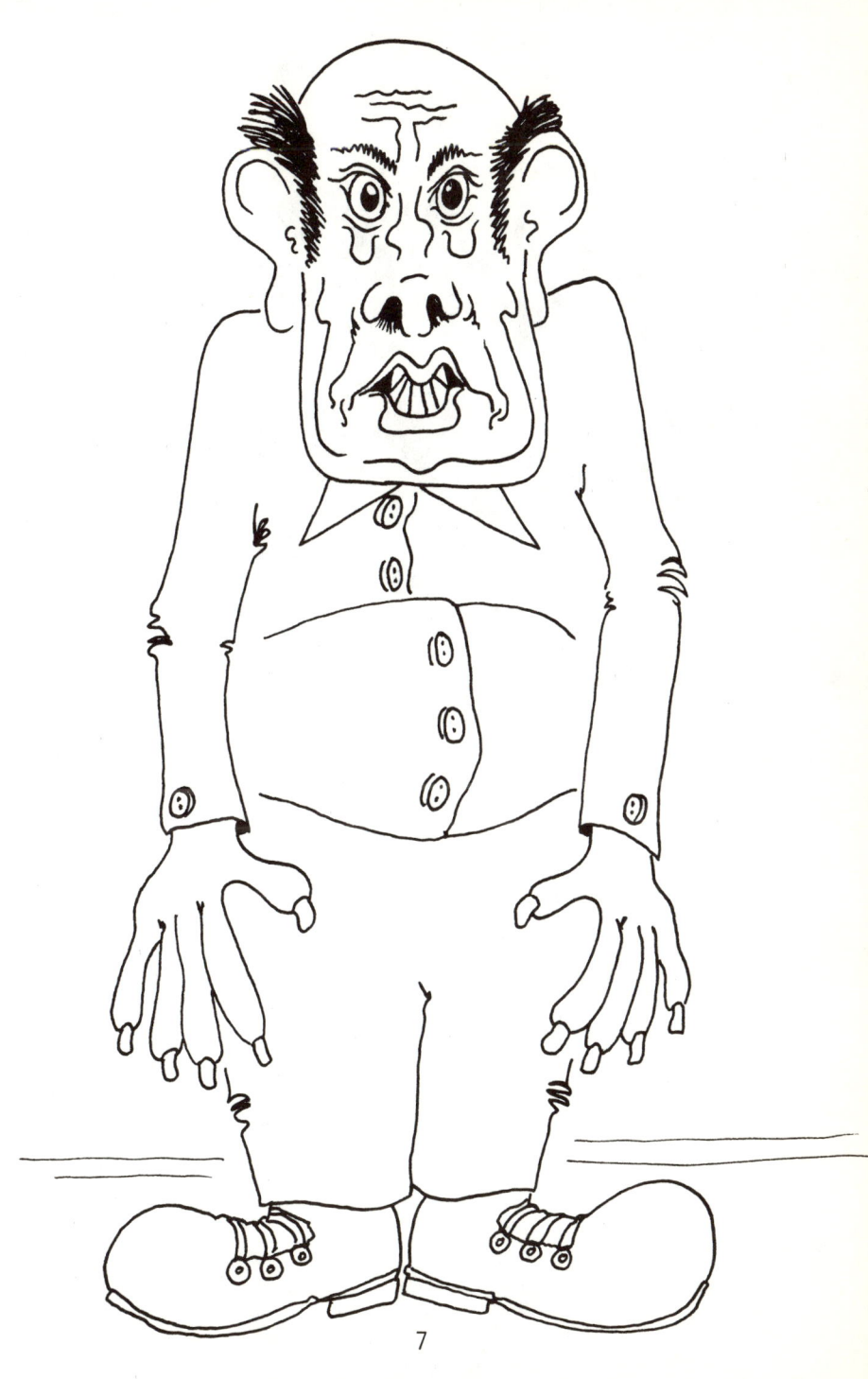

NO SLED

I wanted to go sledding
But I didn't have a sled,
So my Mom said that I should use
A big old plastic bag instead.

But I didn't hear her say "plastic",
So I used the neighbor lady.

MINCEMEAT PIE

Today I ate a mincemeat pie.
"It's good!! What's in it?", wondered I.
So I got my Mom's old fashioned cookbook
And flipped through the pages to take a look.

You need lots of beef, lean and ground,
And a bunch of raisins, about a pound.
Take the very best oranges you can find,
And very carefully grate the rind.
Throw in a lemon and an apple too,
And some coriander, just a dab'll do.
Now add some salt and cinnamon to it,
Some allspice, and cloves, and a little beef suet.
Grab some dried currants and sugar brown,
And pour some orange juice and brandy on.
Wrap it all up in a tender crust.
Then bake it, and serve it, and eat 'til ya bust!!

SARA

There was a girl named Sara.
For short they called her "Sair".
She always came to school
With a flower in her hair.

Then one day she came with two.
The next day, three. Then four!
And every day thereafter
She came with more and more!!

In one class I sat behind her,
And I looked close at Sair,
And it looked to me that with the flowers
There were some weeds in there.

And I think I saw a hoe in there,
And some sprinklers, and a rake,
And I saw some creepy-crawly things!
GOOD GRIEF!! How much could one guy take??!!

So I ran and told the teacher,
And she quickly grabbed ol' Sair
And rushed her to the shower room
To make her wash her hair.

And now Sair's hair is regular.
It's just like yours and mine.
Once in awhile she wears a flower,
But no longer all the time.

So, little girls, remember
Everyday to wash your hair!
Scrub, and clean, and brush it,
Or you'll wind up like Sair.

Cuz I don't ever want to see,
From now until I'm dead,
Another person in the whole, wide world
With a garden on her head!!

BILL EEGOTE

Bill Eegote was a real ninny.
The ninniest of the nin!
No matter who you're talkin' to
He'd always butt right in.

You could be discussin' politics,
Or law, or medicine,
And along would come that Bill Eegote
And just start buttin' in.

One day two shepherds were yakkin' on
Just how to raise their flock.
Ol' Bill Eegote came buttin' in
And wouldn't let them talk.

One shepherd got disgusted
And said, "Just you wait and see!!
I'm teachin' you a lesson
Not to butt right in on me!!"

And he went and got his billy goat
And said to Bill Eegote, "Bend down!"
Then he had his goat butt Billy's butt
'Til he knocked him back to town.

So, Bill Eegote learned his lesson.
I hope you've learned it too,
Or I'll have that shepherd get his goat
And butt right in on you!

LOVELY DAY

It was a beautiful day today.
The sun wiz worm and brightt.
There wuz a rainbiw in the sku.
Whrt a rewlly beautifil sight!!

The clouds wepe soft and flufgy
And therf was a gentll breeeees.
And the birfs were singing sewetly
Way op im the treez.

I walked down by our liffle brook.
The woter wiz cuul and clear.
The fosh were jimping all arounf.
Downstrean thare wert somf deer.

The flowerd wert dancinf im tha wind.
The frogs wert rewlly croakin'.
I8d lyke to writf somf more,
But I timk me typrittar ix brokin'.

THE BURGER

The waitress said, "Order please".
I said, "Gimme a burger with a slice of cheese,
And I want it on a sesame bun,
And please could you make it very well done?
And put on some lettuce, crispy and clean,
And a bunch of dill pickles, juicy and green,
And mustard, and catsup, and mayonaise,
And lots of bacon, carefully braised,
And mushrooms, and peppers, and onions fried,
And an order of french fries on the side,
And make it snappy! I'm dyin' to try it!

AW SHUCKS!! I forgot!! I'm on a diet!!"

RED PAINT

There's a can of paint upon a shelf
In the corner of my shop.
Inside that can are hundreds and hundreds
Of little red drippety-drops.

Do you s'pose those little red drippety-drops,
Once they've gotten aquainted,
Are talkin' to each other about
The places they might soon be painted?

Maybe one wants to be on a fire truck
All polished, and shiney, and clean.
One wants to be on the side of a barn,
And another on a can marked "gasoline".

And one wants to go on a round-the-world cruise,
Painted on the side of a ship.
And one says she'd like to wind up on the floor
As a plain old simple old drip.

Maybe one's sayin', "Hey, I wanna be
The red on a toy clown's nose".
And another one's sayin' he doesn't care
Where in the world he goes.

And one wants to be right in the middle
Of the hood of a brand new car.
And one wants to be on a Christmas tree,
Up top on a bright red star.

Yeah, I'll bet those little red drippety-drops
Are plottin', and plannin', and dreamin'.
I think I'll open up that can
And listen right in on their schemin'.

So, I opened up that can of red paint,
And do you know what was goin' on inside?

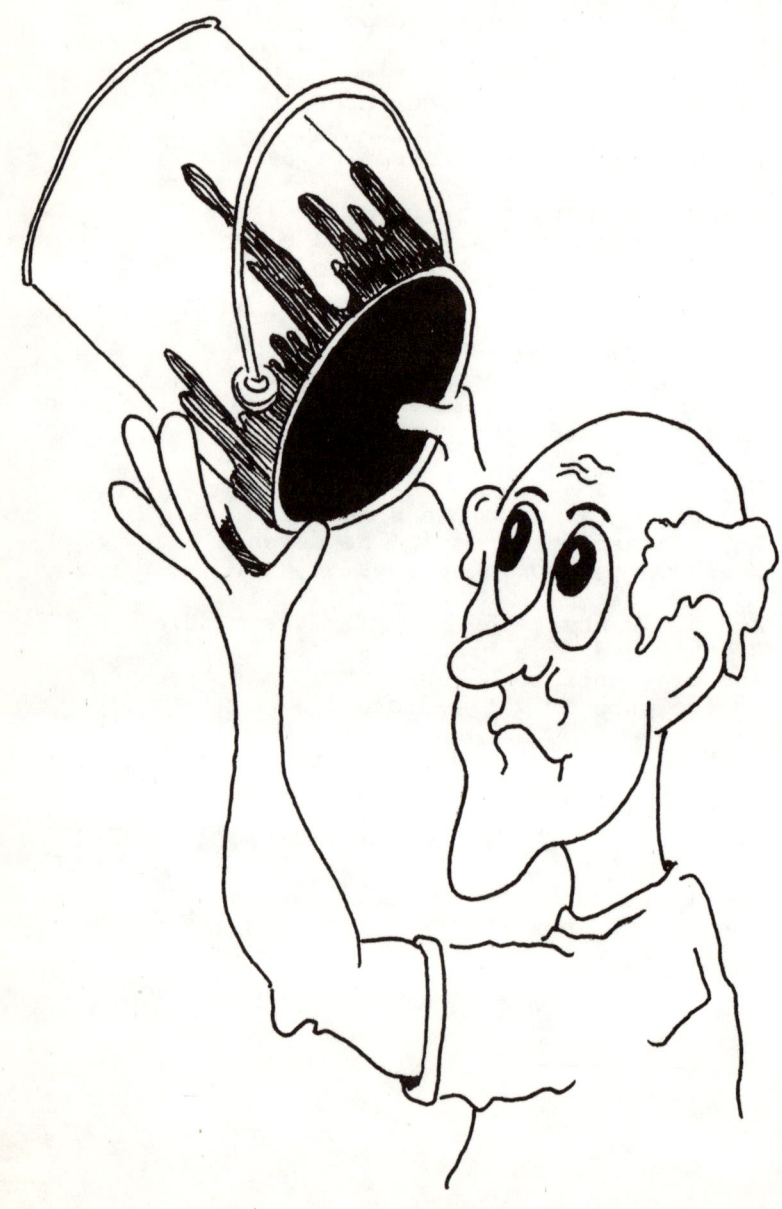

THE CATS

Carol had a lovely cat.
She decided to name him Brandy.
He was well bred, and really cute.
As cats go, he's a dandy.

Jerry's cat was Alexander.
For short they called him Al.
Jerry'd play with Al all day.
Al was really Jerry's pal.

One day the cats were wrestling
On the counter near the blender.
They rolled in....click....whir....
Gurgle....mix....Brandy Alexander!!!

OUT AND IN

When you go outside
  Do you enter the out,
  Or do you exit the in?
Does it matter most
  Where you're going, or
  Does it matter where you've been?

Or is it that when you exit
  You're going into the out?
  Or else it maybe could be
That when you go in
  You exit the out.
  It's a mystery to me!!!

WHAT TO DO! WHAT TO DO!

I don't know what to do today.
No one else is home.
If I could think of something
Maybe I'd write a poem.

Or maybe I could watch TV,
Or go and stand on my head,
Or maybe I could take a nap,
But I'd rather write a poem instead.

OH! I just did!!

SHE LOVES ME, SHE LOVES ME NOT

THE BAKER

>She loafs me.
>She loafs me not.

THE HIGH JUMPER

>She leaps me.
>She leaps me not.

THE MUSICIAN

>She loves me.
>She loves my note.

MAN FROM NORTH DAKOTA

>She loves me.
>She loves Minot.

THE BODY BUILDER

>She lifts me.
>She lifts me not.

THE YES MAN

>She loves me.
>She loves my nod.

THE BOXER

>She gloves me.
>She gloves me not.

MAN WITH INSECT COLLECTION

>She loves me.
>She loves my gnat.

THE EAR DOCTOR

>She lobes me.
>She lobes me not.

THE COMEDIAN

>She laughs me.
>She laughs me not.

THE TREE SURGEON

>She leafs me.
>She leafs me not.

THE BOY SCOUT

>She loves me.
>She loves my knot.

BUTCH'S BOY

There was a little boy
Whose father's name was Butch.
He was a little brat.
Nobody liked him much.
He'd break his toys.
He'd fight with boys.
He'd pull the little girl's hair.
He'd throw his food.
He was no good,
No matter when or where.

He was Butch's boy, remember?
And nobody liked him much.
In fact, they always called him
A regular son-of-a-butch.

GREAT IDEA

I have a great idea!
Should I tell you what I think?
Well, I would, but I can't today.
My pen is running out of ink.

THE MONSTER

There's a monster under my bed.
I just know he's hiding there.
He has fourteen beady eyes
And he's covered with curly hair.
I can hear him growl when the lights go out,
And I just know that he's really mean.
And I just know that he's big and he's ugly,
Even though he's never been seen.

I just know he's hiding under my bed
Waiting for me to doze.
Then he'll come crawling out
And bop me on the nose,
And bite my neck with his long, sharp fangs,
And screech some horrible sound,
And tie my arms and legs in knots,
And smash me all around.

I just know he's hiding under my bed.
Whatever shall I do???

AHA!! ....sneak....tip-toe.....poke.....
"Hey Mom, may I sleep with Dad and you?????"

GETTING UP

If you get up in the morning
And stub your toe on the edge of the bed,
And bend over to put your slippers on
And find a headache in your head,
And if you stretch your arms out
And scratch your knuckles on the wall,
And then walk into the other room
And slip on the puppy's ball,
And if you discover the toothpaste is empty,
And you're out of coffee too,
And your favorite shirt is in the wash,
And there's no clean socks for you,
And if you look into the mirror
And see your eyes are bloodshot red,
Don't even try to make it.
Just pull the shades and go back to bed.

THE GURNK

In our house, down in the cellar,
There's a Gurnk that's living there.
I hear him squeal, and snort, and growl
Everytime I'm on the stair.

I don't know if he's big or small,
Or if he's mean or nice.
But one thing, with that Gurnk down there,
We don't have any mice.

THE BASKETBALL GAME

1st quarter

I was open for a slam-dunk
If Bill would have passed to me.
But before the pass, he traveled,
According to the referee.

2nd quarter

I was open for a slam-dunk
If Jeff would have passed to me.
But before the pass, he double-dribbled,
According to the referee.

3rd quarter

I was open for a slam-dunk
If Sam would have passed to me.
But before the pass, he stepped out-of-bounds,
According to the referee.

4th quarter

I was open for a slam-dunk
If Bob would have passed to me.
But before the pass, he went over-and-back,
According to the referee.

After the game

When the game was over, I wasn't angry
With Bob, or Sam, or Bill, or Jeff.
But before I left the basketball floor,

I slam-dunked the ref.

FRED BROWN

Freddie Brown
Went to town
To try to buy a frown.
The clerk said,
"I'm sorry Fred.
I have no wrinkles for your head."

So ....being wise..........
Fred glued a prune between his eyes.

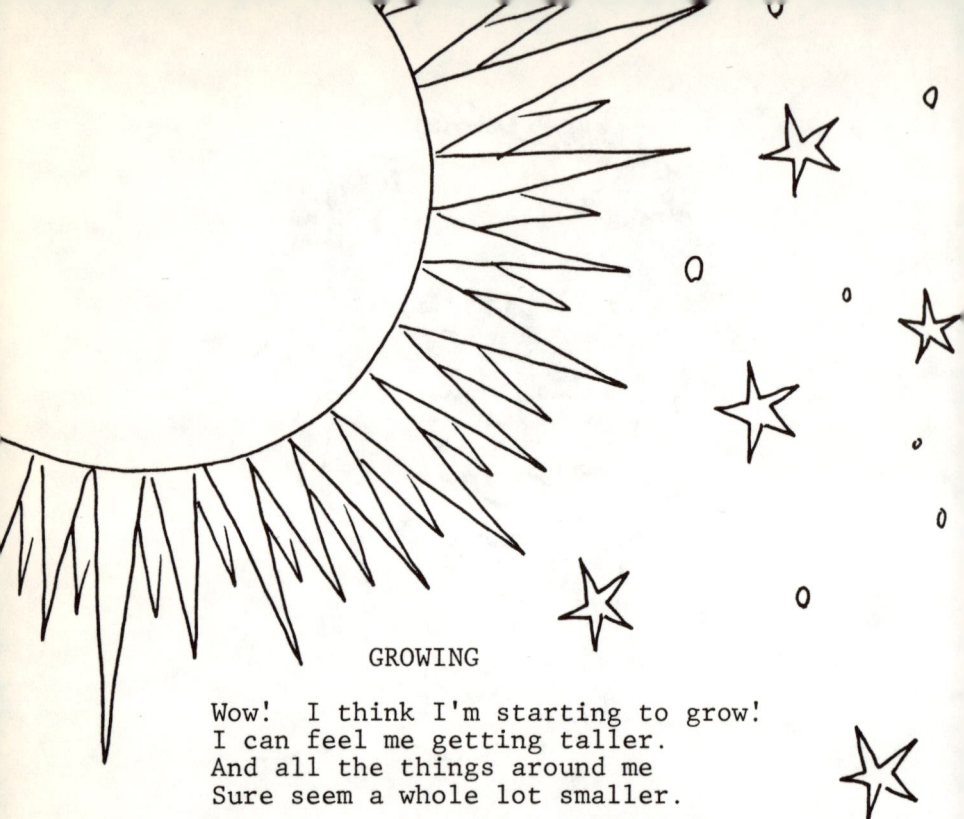

GROWING

Wow! I think I'm starting to grow!
I can feel me getting taller.
And all the things around me
Sure seem a whole lot smaller.

Whoops! I just bumped my head
On the branch of a pretty big tree.
Good gosh! I'm really growing!
What will become of me?!

Holy cow! I just stuck my head
Through a big white fluffy cloud.
And a rocket just brushed past my nose.
Boy!! Was it ever loud!

And now the planets are twirling by.
This is really sort of fun!
But now it's getting really warm!
Yup!! Here comes the sun!!

It's strange to be so very tall!
My head's in space. My feet are on sod.
And I'm still getting taller!
Oh, my goodness!!!

Hello, God!

BIG-EARRED BINSKI

Binski had the biggest ears
Of any dog on Earth.
And everyone would stop to ask,
"How much is that dog worth?"

It's easy to place a value
On a horse, or cat, or pig.
But how can you set a price
On a dog with ears so big?

FOOTBALL

When I was a little kid
My father said to me,
"All the while you're growing up
Be the best that you can be."
He said, "Work very hard in school,
And learn everything you can,
And be sure to go out for football
Or you'll only be half-a-man.
Football will make a man of you.
It'll make you tough and wise.
Don't be half-a-man, my son,
Like so many other guys."

So I remembered my father's words,
And when school opened that fall,
In order not to be half-a-man
I signed up to play football.
Ya, football would make a man of me.
That's what my father said.
But strange things happened in those games,
And I'm lucky I'm not dead.

One great big guy tackled me
And tore off one of my hands.
Another guy ripped my arm off
And threw it in the stands.
While I was running really fast
On my favorite pass route,
A fat guy hit me in the face
And knocked half my teeth right out.
Then one game, while blocking,
I got tripped. As I fell down
Someone punted my leg off
Before I even hit the ground.
And I got an eye poked out,
And they tore an ear off too.
The coach just said, "Don't worry kid!
We're makin' a man of you."

Well, I did the very best I could
And followed my father's plan.

33

But somehow I still wound up to be
Only half-a-man.

THE SEEING-EYE DOG

Old man Galley was going blind
So he bought a seeing-eye dog.
Then he got around just fine
Through the rain, and the snow, and the fog.

But, one day the dog went blind.
Old Galley would need a new plan.
However, the dog solved the problem.

He bought a seeing-eye man.

BETTY LOU AND BERTHA

Betty Lou was a real beauty,
Prettier than a fresh-picked flower.
The secret to her lovely looks
Was her periodic self-improvement hour.

She'd file her nails, and polish them too,
And scrub her dimply little dimples,
And shave her legs 'til they were smooth,
And pop her pimply little pimples,
And floss her teeth until they squeaked,
And pluck her eyebrows one by one,
And wash her hair and curl it too,
And keep on primping until she was done.

When she finished, she was quite a sight,
All gorgeous, and pretty, and cute.
No one lovlier could be found.
Her self-improvement hour made her a beaut.

But Bertha was a real hag.
In fact, she had such an ugly beak
That to be half as cute as Betty Lou
She'd need a self-improvement week.

MERLIN'S BIRDHOUSE

Merlin bought a birdhouse,
But the holes were much too big.
No birds moved in because of this.
The first tenant was a pig.
And then a green giraffe moved in,
And then a yellow horse,
And then a herd of wildebeests,
And then a cow, of course, ...
Next, a pink rhinocerous,
And then a gray, old moose,
And then a stripeless zebra,
And then an orange mongoose.

Too many weird things in his yard,
This would never do.
So Merlin boxed it up one day
And gave it to the zoo.

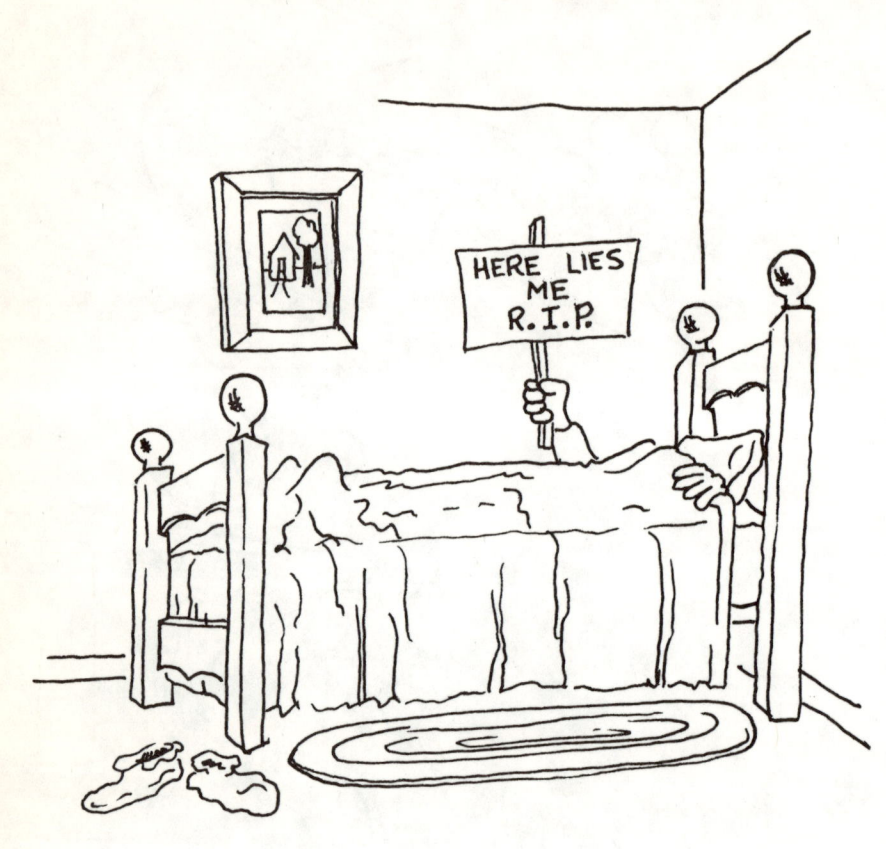

GETTING TO SLEEP

So, ... you can't get to sleep?
Don't lie there and weep!
Just pull some covers up over your head,
And then pretend that you're dead!

THE ELEPHANT AND THE ANT

An elephant was out for a stroll,
And as I stood by and watched
I saw an ant walking in his path.
I closed my eyes and heard a SPLOTCH!!

I ran over there as fast as I could
As a big crowd gathered around.
The ant just kept walkin' along!!
A flat elephant was squished on the ground!!

How could the ant survive, you ask?
How could such a thing be?
Well, ...

..... it was a midget elephant
And a giant ant, you see!

THE BOTTLE

We found a fancy bottle
In a hole in a big old tree.
My sister said it might be magic
So we took it home to see.

She said if we would rub it
A Genie might come out,
And then he'd grant three wishes
To each of us, no doubt.

So I rubbed, and rubbed, and rubbed it.
I shouldn't have listened to my dumb sister!
No Genie came out of that bottle,
And all I got was a blister!!

THE PASTA MACHINE

    This morning I decided I needed to lose some weight, so I planned to eat less for a few days to see if I could peel off a few pounds.
    This afternoon Jerry came over and brought his pasta machine.
We made Linguine pasta,
And Spaghetti pasta,
And Ragatoni pasta,
And Fetacini pasta,
And Manicotti pasta,
And Lasagne pasta,
And Amorini pasta,
And Fusilli pasta,
And Stivaletti pasta,
And Vermicelli pasta,
And Stelline pasta,
And it was all very, very, very, very good, and all afternoon and all night we ate pasta, and ate more pasta, and more pasta. We ate pasta until it was coming out of our ears.
    If we keep doin' this, how am I pasta lose any weight??

THE GUN CLEANER

There was an old hunter named Eiffel.
One day he was cleaning his rifle.
It went off with a boom
And destroyed the whole room.
If that didn't kill him, his wife'll.

LYNN

Lynn bought two weird fish.
Both fish were finless.
She was a pitcher in softball.
In twenty games she was winless.
Her favorite hotdogs were the
Ones that were skinless.
She never smiled much.
Her face was grinless.
She rarely drank alcohol.
Her diet was ginless.
Her last relative died,
Which left her kinless.
Her house had no entrance.
The building was inless.
She was very nice.
She was actually sinless.
But, she got really fat,
Which made her thinless,
And her boyfriend, Quin, left her,
Which left her Quinless,
So she died, heartbroken,
Which left the world Lynnless.

APPLIANCES

We have a 'lectric mixer,
And a 'lectric toaster too,
And a 'lectric popcorn popper
To pop some corn for you.
We have a 'lectric stove
For cookin' all our food.
We have a 'lectric TV set
To watch if you're in the mood.
We have a 'lectric radio,
And a 'lectric saw and drill,
And 'lectric lamps and heaters
And a 'lectric barbecue grill.
We have a 'lectric can opener,
And outlets in the wall,
And if we ever get 'lectricity
We'll be able to use them all.

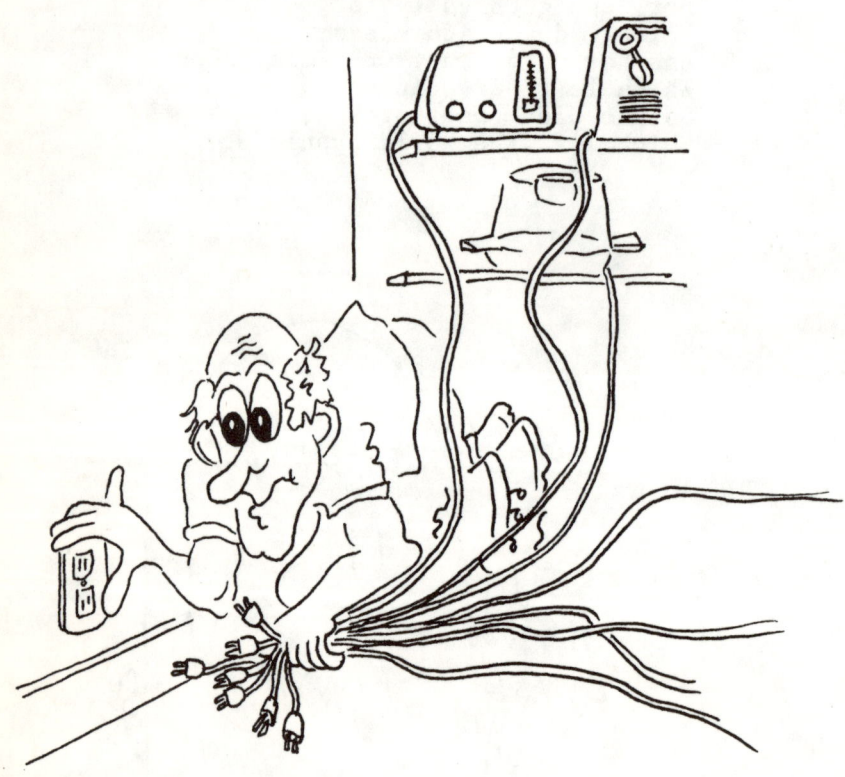

BEDRIDDEN

One night I got ready for bed
And put my pajamas on.
Then I crawled between the sheets,
And after a nice long yawn

I fell asleep.

I started to dream about getting ready for bed,
And I was putting my pajamas on.
Then I crawled between the sheets again,
And after a nice long yawn

I fell asleep again.
Well, I woke up the next morning,

And I've been in bed ever since,
And I'm sure I'll be here 'til Lord knows when.
Cuz, since I fell asleep twice that night
I'm stayin' here 'til I wake up again.

PROFESSIONS

Golda owns a jewelry store.
Teddy makes stuffed bears.
Egbert runs a chicken farm.
Harry is a barber.
Frank sells hotdogs.
Sue is a lawyer.
Melody writes songs.

John doesn't want to grow up
and get a job.
He's afraid he'll have to be a toilet!!

GOING DEAF

I ran home from school to change my clothes.
I couldn't wait to get out to play.
We were going to build a snowman
On this chilly, windy day.

When I went into the kitchen
My Mom said something to me,
But I only saw her lips move.
What could the problem be?

I rushed into the livingroom.
Sis was dancing all around.
I was sure the music must be on
But I couldn't hear a sound.

I ran outside into the street
And there wasn't a sound out there.
Not a honk, or screech, or zoom, or roar,
Not a bit of noise anywhere!!

I figured I must be going deaf
So I ran to the end of the block.
That's where our local clinic was.
I hurried in to see the doc.

The doctor took one look at me
And said, "Oh you crazy fool!

You forgot to take your earmuffs off
When you came home from school!!"

BOUNCING BABY BOY

A brand new bouncing baby boy
Was born to Betty and Boris BaCall.
What would they do with a bouncing boy?
Should they use him for a basketball?

No. Not this brand new baby boy.
He's just much too fat.
Cuz when they try to bounce him
He simply makes a SPLAT!!

THE CIDER

The cider was brought to the county fair.
Each jug was given a letter.
"A" cider, "B" cider, "C" cider, "D" cider,....
The judges would choose the better.

Now old Ma Schneider entered her cider.
Her cider was really fantastic.
She knew that only the "B" cider could beat her.
To win she must do something drastic!

Later, the jug marked "B" was stolen.
Oh no!! Good gosh!! Good grief!!
Who could have done such a terrible thing?
Someone yelled, "Ma Schneider's the thief!"

Ma ran with the jug tucked under her arm
Through the woods, and the swamp, and the bog.
She ran 'til she couldn't run anymore,
Then she rested herself on a log.

She placed the jug of "B" cider beside her,
And when the mob came runnin' in
She drank it up fast, hid the jug in the bushes,
And just sat there with a grin.

"Why is she grinnin'?", someone asked.
"We know she swiped the "B" cider."
But old Ma knew that they couldn't prove it
With the evidence now hidden inside her.

So they all returned to the fair
To judge the rest of the juice.
And old Ma Schneider was jumpin' with joy,
Cuz with "B" gone she just couldn't lose.

So did Ma Schneider's cider win at the fair?
With "B" gone, hers was the best!!
Well, we'll never know, cuz in all the commotion
Some other thief stole all the rest.

THE CANNIBAL DINNER

Two cannibals came knockin'
On my door the other night.
They held me down, and with some ropes
They tied me really tight.

They took me to their kitchen
And got out their recipe book.
I didn't know just what to expect,
But I didn't like the way things looked.

They began to prepare their dinner,
And it was very easy to see
That the groceries for their evening meal
Were going to be me!!

From my hair they made a salad,
And some soup from my big toes.
They used my eyes for hard-boiled eggs,
And made a sandwich from my nose.

My ears became two cookies.
My shoulders made a roast.
My fingers were used for toothpicks.
They used my hands for toast.

My thumbs became two hotdogs.
They made jello from my knees.
My chin became their doggy's bone.
From my brain they made some cheese.

This all was very painful!
Boy, did I ever squeal!
It was no fun at all to be
Somebody else's meal.

So, there I was in pots and pans
Scattered all about the room.
How would I get out of there?
I'd better do it soon!

Well, ... I really was quite nervous!
This was certainly a scare!
So, ... I just pulled myself together
And ran right out of there!

THE NAME CHANGE

There was a girl named Patty L.
She was not feeling very well.
The doc eventually found out why,
And he amputated her letter "y".

So Patty L. became Patt L.,
But if you knew her you could tell
That now she was feeling sad.
What made her feel so very bad?

Well, she missed her little letter "y",
So she went out to try to buy
A brand new "y" made just for her.
Then things could be just as they were.

She looked high, and she looked low,
But no matter where it was she'd go
She could not find a letter "y"
Regardless how hard it was she'd try.

So she bought a little "i" on sale,
And that will end this little tale.
It serves her very, very well,
And now she's known as Patti L.

THE FRENCH FRY STEALERS

When you go to a restaurant
And order yourself some fries,
Sometimes you have to guard 'em
From all the other guys.

There's the guy who's with you in the booth
Who didn't feel like eatin'.
But when YOUR fries come, he digs in.
You'd like to give him a beatin'!

There's the friend of yours who walks on by
And stops for awhile to chat.
While she's chattin' she grabs a few.
You'd like to give her a swat!

And when they steal 'em, they always take
The very best ones from you.
They take the long ones. They take the crisp ones.
And they take your catsup too.

The next time someone steals my fries,
Whether the soggy ones or the best,
I'm gonna jump right up and grab 'em
And make a citizen's arrest.

LEE AND I

Lee and I loved the Fourth of July.
We enjoyed it tremendously.
We bought a lot of fireworks
And played on endlessly,
'Til Lee sat on a firecracker.
Now we call him "Endless Lee".

THE EARTH SAVER

Just at dawn this morning
I awoke to some horrible sounds.
There were spaceships flying everywhere
Carrying aliens Earthbound.

I knew I had to shoot 'em down
Before they captured you and me,
So I zinged, and zapped, and zonged at them,
And fought on fearlessly.

All day long I battled them,
And just before nightfall
I finally won the skirmish.
I had beaten them one and all.

And when the fight was over
They surrendered. I was the winner.

Then I shut off the video game,
And went in the kitchen for dinner.

SKREK

Sometimes you get really tired
Of playin' with your toys,
So you get up a good old game
Of Indians and cowboys.

Lance and I were the cowboys, SKREK
So we went to get our guns. SKREK
Molly and Jan were the Indians. SKREK
We were going to have some fun. SKREK

Jan and Molly went to hide. SKREK
Then we'd try to find 'em. SKREK
Our plan was simply to follow their tracks, SKREK
And then sneak up behind them. SKREK

Lance went first, then I followed, SKREK
And we tramped through the neighborhood. SKREK
But something definitely musta been wrong. SKREK
As cowboys we weren't too good. SKREK

We looked in bushes. We looked in trees. SKREK
We looked here and there. SKREK
We looked all over for Jan and Molly, SKREK
But we couldn't find 'em anywhere. SKREK

Then I discovered what was wrong. SKREK
The trouble was with Lance. SKREK
You can't sneak up on Indians SKREK
When your partner's wearin' corduroy pants. SKREK

BOBBY FEEGLE

Little Bobby Feegle
Stole a little beagle,
Threw rocks at a seagull,
Shot at an eagle,

And he was arrested
Cuz it all was illegal.

MY FROG

Once I owned a bullfrog.
He was very round and plump.
I put him on a diet
So he could learn to jump.

I fed him only ant legs
With a few mosquito beaks,
And I kept him on that diet
For about a couple of weeks.

When he had lost his weight
We practiced really hard.
We built a little jumping ring
Right out in our back yard.

Soon my frog was ready.
There was no one he could not beat.
Shucks! Without even tryin' hard
He could jump a hundred feet.

So I entered him in competition
To be held on Saturday.
He was ready, I was sure,
To be the champ of the USA.

The day before the contest
We relaxed and laughed and joked.
But he didn't win the championship,
Cuz Friday night he croaked.

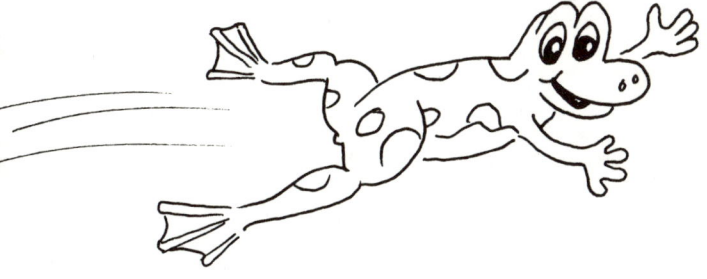

WHO COULD LOVE A WART HOG?

Who in the world could love a wart hog?
Nobody thinks very much of 'em.
They're such ugly, unshapely, despicable things
That even their mothers don't love 'em.

They're smelly, and dirty, and fat,
And they're covered with lumpety bumps.
Their disposition is not very good.
Most of 'em are really big grumps.

But if everyone said you were smelly and fat
And too ugly for even the zoo,
You'd prob'ly be mean and cantankerous
And a real grumpety old grump too.

You see, ...even if wart hogs are ugly,
They still have some feelings inside.
And the saddest thing you could ever have seen
Is if you've seen a wart hog that's cried.

One day I saw a wart hog cryin'.
It seemed that his tears would not end.
So I asked, "What's wrong?", and he told me.
He said, "All I need is a friend".

He said, "All my life no one has loved me,
And no one ever cares how I feel.
But deep down inside I'm a pretty good guy.
I can be friendly, and nice, and genteel".

So I hung around that wart hog awhile,
And we talked, and we laughed, and we played,
And we shared some stories of days gone on by,
And we ate picnic lunch in the shade.

I discovered that wart hogs aren't quite so bad,
That they feel and they care just like I do.
So, who in the world could love a wart hog?
Well, I'll tell you.   Me! That's who!!

MR. TOG AND MR. NOCT

Early every morning,
Just before the dawn,
Mr. Tog goes runnin' 'round
And puts the colors on.

He makes the sky a shade of blue.
And clouds?? He makes them white.
He makes the grass all shades of green.
Then he colors the flowers bright.

He makes the birds all different colors,
And he puts the gold in rings.
He runs around like crazy
And colors every single thing.

Then, just when the sun goes down,
Mr. Noct makes everything black.
But don't worry, cuz before morn
Mr. Tog will put the colors back.

BIG BILL

Bill was seven-foot-six and weighed 335.
He played center on the basketball team.
He'd glide through the air and slam the ball in.
Bill could score anytime, it seemed.

On the basketball floor, no one could stop him.
His equal could not be found.
There was no doubt in anyone's mind
That by far he was the best around.

But one day there happened a terrible thing.
He fell down and broke his leg, ...OUCH !!
A wheel-chair big enough couldn't be found,

So they built him a giant wheel-couch.

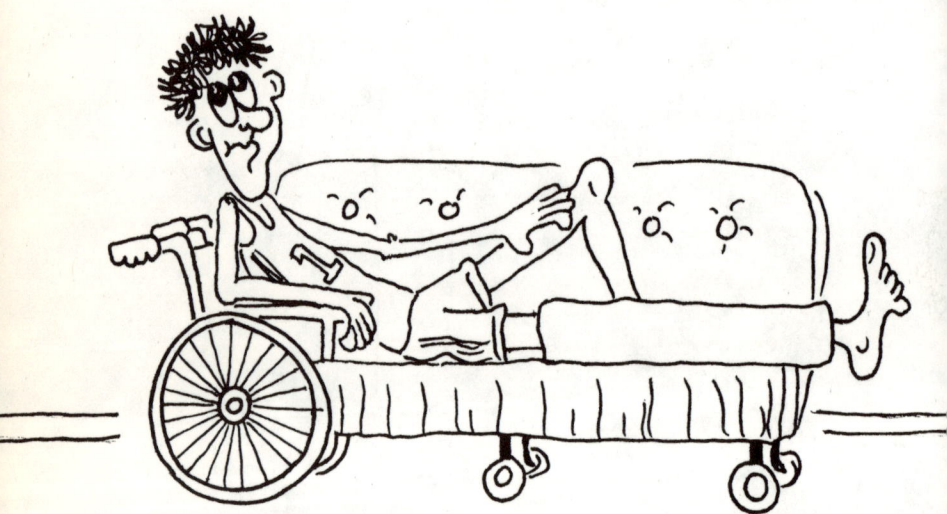

OUR TOWN

Whatever your town might be like,
Ours is prob'ly just the same.
Except that in our little town
Everyone has a weird name.
Chuck Olot runs the candy store.
Frank Furter owns the hotdog stand.
Abel Ringer works at the church.
Con Ductor leads the local band.
Luke Warm runs the water works.
Phil Erup owns the station.
Cal Ifornya moved away
To the western part of the nation.
Reverend Chris Chen is our clergyman.
Bill Bord --- our advertiser.
Sam Sonite runs the travel bureau.
The brewery owner? Bud Wizer.
Gordon Bleu and Jeff Salad
Own the cafe on the corner.
Mike Rafone is our local DJ.
Kitty Litter is the pet shop owner.
Miles Toorun is quite a jogger,
And if you think that's strange,
Morgan Shotts and Rick Oshay
Work at the rifle range.
Lee Mealone is a real hermit.
Doug Ahole is our grave digger.
Annette Full is a fisherwoman.
No one catches 'em bigger.
Cliff Climber lives up in the hills.
Steve Adore works on the docks.
Sparkie Plug is our mechanic.
Al Arm fixes all our clocks.
Amber Gris owns a perfume store.
Curt En runs a drapery shop.
Ann Twerp moved to Belgium.
Cherry Soda sell us pop.
Yes, our names are really different.
You'll find no Smiths or Jones.
And down there at the local bank
Buck Lender makes the loans.
Our telegraph man just passed away.
He was getting very old.
You can have the job. You can start today,
If your name is Morris Code.

THE SKINNY PIG

Once there was a skinny pig.
Her name was Merilee.
She sang, and danced, and shouted,
"They'll get no ham from me.

And they'll get no bacon either,
For I'm much too thin, you see,
And they'll get no chops or sausage.
There's no need to butcher me."

So she never ate a single thing,
And she drank only diet pop.
Her goal was to simply stay alive
And escape the butcher shop.

She stayed as skinny as she could.
A long life was her ambition.
But, alas her dreams were thwarted.
She died of malnutrition.

QUESTIONS ALL PARENTS SHOULD BE ABLE TO ANSWER

Where does the log go
    after the fire?
How can a voice go
    through a phone wire?
Where does the light go
    when it gets dark?
Why don't dogs go "meow"
    and kittens go "bark"?
How do you get back
    on a street that's one way?
Where do the clouds go
    on a sunny day?
Where does the bubble go
    after the burst?
The chicken or the egg,
    which came first?
How come denim pants aren't
    called "Ralphs" insteada "Jeans"?
And if cows eat grass
    how come milk isn't green?
If a nickel is bigger
    why's it less than a dime?
And why the heck is it
    that poems have to rhyme?

THE INVESTMENT

Once, long ago, the Nunyer children,
Bess, Lou, Myrtle, and Thor,
Wanted to make some money,
So they bought themselves a store.

The customers came flockin' in,
Each day more and more.
And so with all their profits
They bought another store.

And they made so very much money
That they continued to expand.
They bought more stores from coast to coast
And spread throughout the land.

A catchy name was needed.
They gave the job to Bess.
Ya know what she named their chain of stores?
Well, ...it's "Nunyer Business".

WHAT WOULD YOU SAY IF ..?

What would you say if you were an ant?
"Oh, please don't step on me!" ... SQUISH

What would you say if you were a hanky?
"Please don't blow your nose on me!" ... ISH

What would you say if you were a raindrop?
"I hope I don't land on the sidewalk!" .. SPLAT

What would you say if you were a tire?
"Don't run me over a nail!" .... FLAT

What would you say if you were a car?
"Don't drive me recklessly!" .... CRASH

What would you say if you were a rock?
"Don't throw me in the lake!" .... SPLASH

What would you say if you were a pencil?
"Don't grind me in the sharpener!" ... SKRUNCH

I've thought up a few "what would you says".
Now why don't you think of a bunch?

LITTLE KIDS AND GROWN-UPS

Little kids like merry-go-rounds.
Grown-ups find them boring.
Grown-ups are set in their ways.
Kids have 'maginations soaring.

Little kids do somersaults.
Grown-ups just sit around.
Little kids like to skip and jump.
Grown-ups like their feet on the ground.

Little kids like to scream and cry.
Grown-ups hold it in.
Little kids just play to play.
Grown-ups play to win.

Little kids like lakes for splashin'.
Grown-ups like to wade.
Little kids like wrestlin' in bed.
Grown-ups like beds made.

Grown-ups just watch ball games.
Little kids like playin' ball.
Little kids like juice and pop.
Grown-ups like alcohol.

Grown-ups like cigars and pipes.
Little kids dislike 'em.
Grown-ups just watch footballs fly.
Little kids like to hike 'em.

Kids fool around - Grown-ups work.
Kids like snow - Grown-ups don't.
Kids like runnin' - Grown-ups walk.
Kids will hug you - Grown-ups won't.

Little kids like to laugh and giggle.
Grown-ups mostly seem to frown.
Maybe instead of growing up
We should all be growing down.

SNERBLED NERGS
AND
SKRANGLED BINKS

There are two kinds of people in the world.
Snerbled nergs is one.
They're the ones that are neat to know.
They're the ones that are fun.
Snerbled nergs are friendly,
And they're always very polite.
They go out of their way to please you,
And they never, ever fight.
Snerbled nergs are good listeners,
And they always give good advice.
And if help is what it is you need
You don't have to ask them twice.

And then there are the skrangled binks.
They're not much fun to know.
They're cranky, and moody, and mean,
And they never say a friendly "hello".
They're bullies! They're pushy! They're loud!
They go out of their way to be pests.
And whenever skrangled binks are around
Everyone else is depressed.

Ya wanna know what would be nice?
I'll tell you what methinks.
The world could use more snerbled nergs,
And a lot less skrangled binks.

INDEX

APPLIANCES	48
THE BALLOON	2
THE BASKETBALL GAME	27
BEDRIDDEN	49
BETTY LOU AND BERTHA	37
BIG BILL	67
BIG-EARRED BINSKI	32
BILL EEGOTE	12
BOBBY FEEGLE	62
THE BOTTLE	43
BOUNCING BABY BOY	53
THE BURGER	14
BUTCH'S BOY	22
THE CANNIBAL DINNER	55
THE CATS	17
THE CIDER	54
THE EARTH SAVER	59
THE ELEPHANT AND THE ANT	41
FOOTBALL	33
FRED BROWN	29
THE FRENCH FRY STEALERS	57
GETTING TO SLEEP	40
GETTING UP	25
GOING DEAF	51
THE GRAPEFRUIT SEED	1
GREAT IDEA	23
GROWING	30
THE GUN CLEANER	46
THE GURNK	26
THE INVESTMENT	72
LEE AND I	58
LITTLE KIDS AND GROWN-UPS	74
LOVELY DAY	13
LYNN	47

MELISA'S ROOM	3
MERLIN'S BIRDHOUSE	38
MINCEMEAT PIE	9
THE MONSTER	24
MR. SNOON	6
MR. TOG AND MR. NOCT	66
MY FROG	63
THE NAME CHANGE	56
NO SLED	8
OUR TOWN	69
OUT AND IN	18
THE PASTA MACHINE	44
PROFESSIONS	50
QUESTIONS ALL PARENTS SHOULD BE ABLE TO ANSWER	71
RED PAINT	15
SARA	10
THE SEEING-EYE DOG	35
SHE LOVES ME! SHE LOVES ME NOT!	20
THE SKINNY PIG	70
SKREK	61
SNERBLED NERGS AND SKRANGLED BINKS	75
TOFFEE SQUARES	5
WHAT TO DO! WHAT TO DO!	19
WHAT WOULD YOU SAY IF ....?	73
WHO COULD LOVE A WART HOG?	64

* * * * * * * * * * * * *

For a copy of

"THE GRAPEFRUIT SEED"

send $4.50 plus $1.50 for postage
and handling ($6.00 total) to: